# VOLUME 1: MAROONED

Concept, Story and Art:

COBUS PRINSLOO

Logo design:

THABO MOSHEGO

Assistant line art:

MARK MODIMOLO, THABO MOSHEGO

Advisory panel:

TIM LE ROUX, JOHAN KELLERMAN, SASIKANTH C

Editing: HELENA ENGELBRECHT

Proof reading: JOHAN KELLERMAN, TIM LE ROUX

SPECIAL THANKS TO JURGENS VAN ASWEGEN,
RIAAN GROBLER, KOBUS PRINSLOO, ELIZNA PRINSLOO
AND MY LOYAL TEST SUBJECTS (LOL) — MY FABULOUS
KIDS INA-MARI, MARNO AND FRIENDS FOR THEIR
VALUABLE INPUT IN THIS PROJECT.

**Note on content:** words in the text ending with superscript "G" are defined in the glossary at the end of this book.

By 2550 AD time travel technology has been perfected. This has led to the Time Glider (TG) Project, set up by a consortium of science and engineering agencies from across the world. Its aim is to gain better insight into unclear historical data. The first mission belongs to the TG-1, the spacecraft commanded by professor Patel and his team.

Time Glider Command has one directive: TG teams are assigned to discover and explore, but are under no circumstances allowed to interfere with human history. This may cause uncontrollable ripple effects, jeopardizing the future and even the existence of the Time Glider agency!

## Professor Patel

Commander of the TG-I and co-founder of the International Time Gliders Agency, he is commonly known as "Prof". Born in Kolkata, India, he made a name for his contributions in time travel research. At the age of 25 he already boasted a Nobel prize for his work. His current specialty is the continued research in a potential fifth force in nature, which often keeps him up late at night. His favorite dish, hot lamb curry, helps him to stay awake!

## Liz Ross

Engineer and data analyst. Born and raised on a farm in the USA, she loved to help her dad fix equipment instead of playing with dolls. She loves technology and seems to understand it without having to read a manual! Liz has a special interest in nano-technology and is continuing her studies in this field.

## Deon Dexter

Pilot, and also responsible for Mission Security. With a German father and an Australian mother, Deon is the latest recruit from the International Space Flight Academy and ready for adventure! Deon loves two things more than anything else. Speed – he was a champion of virtual reality racing games from a young age. And challenges, because they lead to new discoveries, inventions and knowledge.

## Quasar

Logistics engineer and timeline navigator. Quasar comes from, well, all over the world. He was conceived in a Japanese robotics laboratory but mainly developed in India. Most of his parts are from China, but he was finally assembled in the USA. With a limited capacity to experience simulated human emotions, he struggles to find his own identity. Quasar's layered artificial neural networks enable him to learn and improve on his programming.

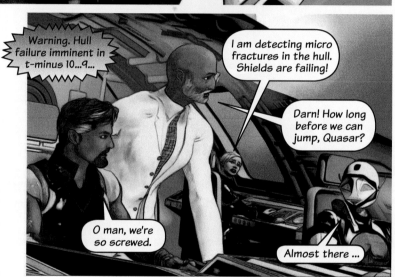

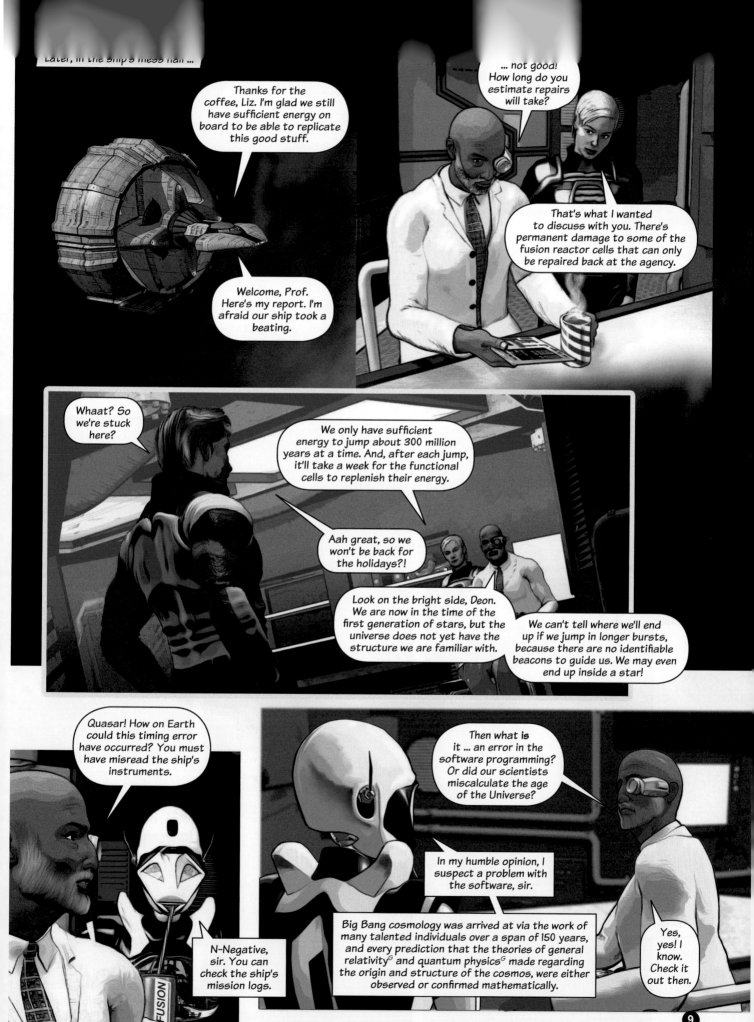

Another science lesson, Prof?

This is fascinating stuff, Deon! The first visual confirmation for an expanding universe was by the great astronomer Edwin Hubble in 1929, after other brilliant scientists like Albert Einstein and Georges Lemaitre had predicted it with their equations of general relativity[G].

But surely he couldn't have observed this in real time?

You have a point. Do yourself a favor and go read up on the doppler effect[G] and the red shift[G] of galaxies' light spectra.

Doppler – as in sound?

Precisely. The same principles also apply to the characteristics of light. But I'm saying no more.

Yes, I just **love** reading.

One time jump later and at long last!

Tha-a-a-at's better! What you see, ladies and gentlemen, is our primordial solar system.

We are now in the Hadean era of Earth's history – about 4 527 million years in the past.

What are those discs around the Sun?

Ah! That confirms the solar nebula[G] hypothesis! That is residue from the original solar nebula, a giant cloud which consisted of hydrogen, helium and heavier elements ejected by the supernovae[G] of other stars.

A nearby shock wave would have made the cloud rotate, and as it began to accelerate, its angular momentum, gravity and inertia would have flattened it into a protoplanetary disk[G]

This is all very interesting, Prof, but can't we take a closer look at Earth?

No way, Deon! It is currently a very violent place, being constantly bombarded with heavy meteor showers and its atmosphere consists of dense gases and interplanetary debris.

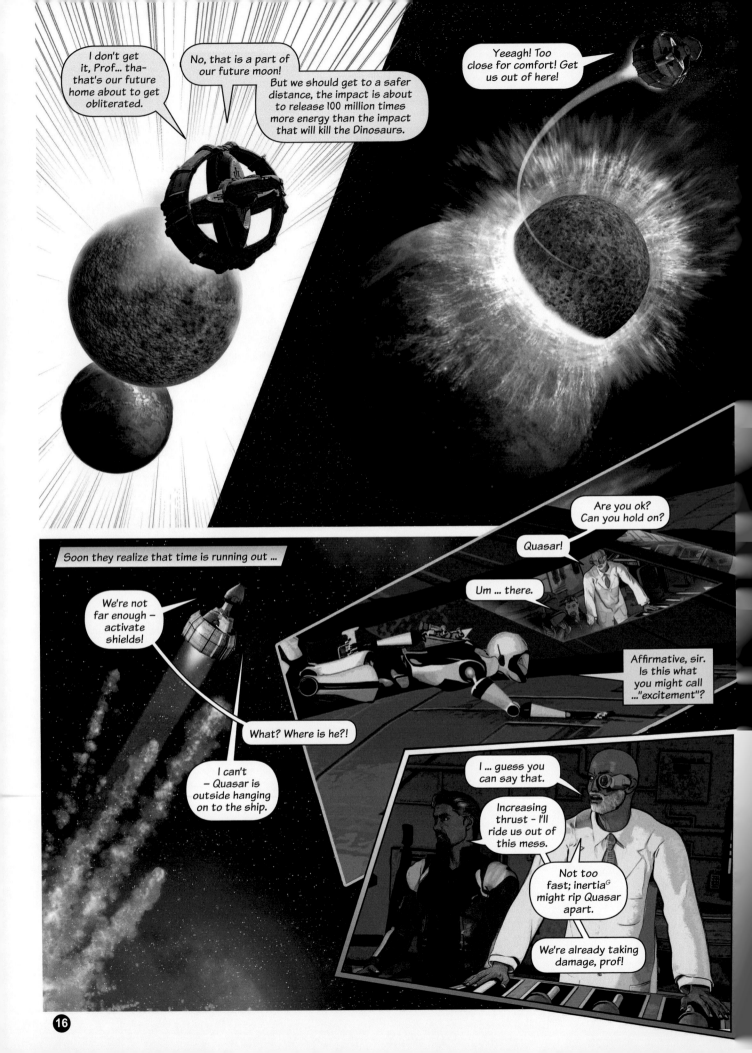

What on Earth happened? I had to hold on for dear life back in my cabin!

Oh, we just avoided getting hit by a part of our future Moon.

What? How come?

Yes Prof, I really think you owe us an explanation!

As Quasar returns to the TG-1, professor Patel continues to explain the moon phenomenon.

The planetoid that just hit Earth is not the actual Moon, but its collision with Earth will contribute to its formation.

You see, the impact just vaporized the Earth's outer mantle and melted both bodies.

A portion of that mantle was ejected into an orbit around it.

I fail to see a new moon in so much devastation.

Not yet, Liz. But in due course, all that ejecta will condense into a single body.

We helped to create our own Moon ... ? That is insane!

No way!

Under the influence of its own gravity, it will form a more spherical body – the Moon!

Hey, look at that concentrated mass – that's the last recorded location of our gravity module.

Well, what do you know! It seems like we may have played a role in kick-starting the creation of our Moon!

But Prof – how did you know that planetoid would be part of our Moon and not a candidate for the destruction of our future world?

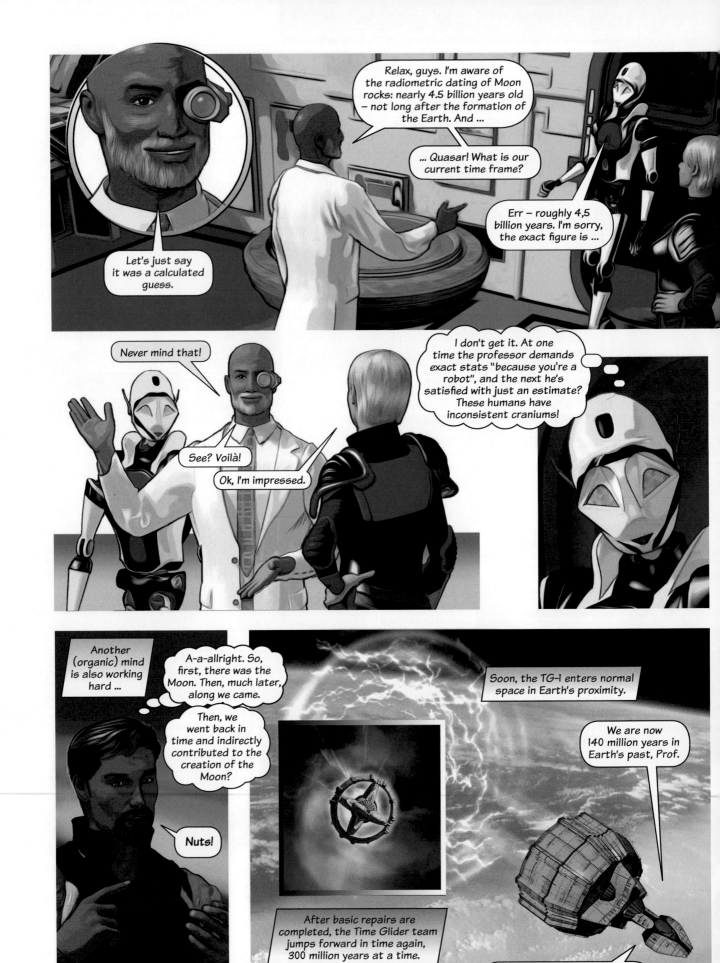

Oh yes! I feel much more at home now. Wait a minute! This doesn't look like Earth.

I don't recognize any continents!

Ahem! Yes, it's not quite our modern Earth – yet. Let me explain.

We are now in the early Cretaceous$^G$ period of Earth's history. What you see are two main continents called Gondwanaland and Laurasia that have split off from an original super continent called Pangea. These are already breaking apart further into the continents we know via a process called "continental drift".

Only after about 35 million years from our present, will Earth look the way we know it.

LAURASIA

GONDWANA

Fascinating! Can we go down and explore?

Hm ... I guess a little detour won't hurt. Let's go check it out!

We have entered Earth's troposphere$^G$, Prof!

Good, but slow down, Deon. Our radar is still offline.

Haha! Seriously, Liz? There's no aircraft around – the sky belongs to us now.

THUMP

What the heck was that?

Seconds later there is a hard bump from outside ...

21

Computer – initiate all safety protocols!

In the meantime, the TG-1 finds itself in the Cretaceous period of Earth's history – about to make an emergency landing after a prehistoric flying reptile hit one of its engines.

Emergency containment fields!

BWAFF!!

The craft skids forward several hundred meters, until it comes to a halt ...

Everybody ok?

Never been better!

I am intact, thanks.

Is this a bad dream?

Darn birds! In modern times they cause plane crashes – now they do it even in prehistoric times!

Too bad our bio scanners are non-operational – otherwise we would have picked up those Quetzalcoatluses in time to prevent a collision!

I'm sorry to say this ... but we have to start work immediately and assess the extent of our predicament.

At least our shields prevented further damage to the craft, but all our sensors are off-line.

Quasar can fly out of gantry 1 and do a sensor sweep of our surroundings before we go outside.

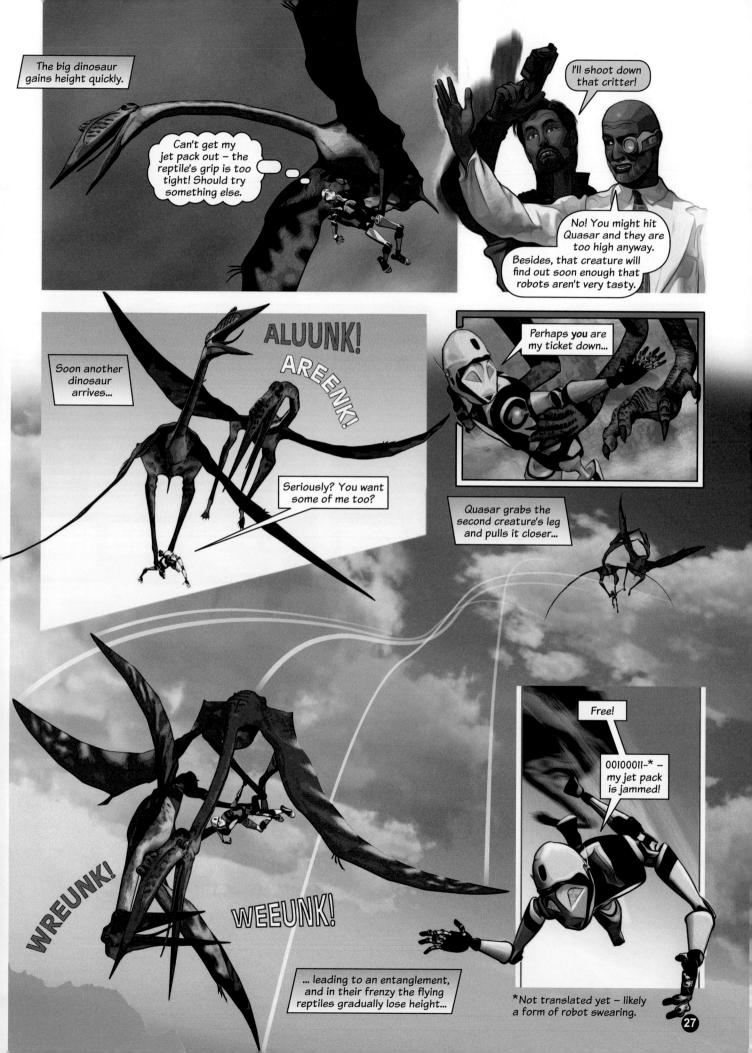

KA-THUDD

Quasar! Are you all right?

And Humpty-Dumpty had a great fall!

Negative. My right thigh is out of its joint.

Give me your hand.

Huh? Gosh, you're falling apart, dude!

Ha-ha. Gotcha!

I *did* give you my hand, didn't I? This is what you humans call "humor" – correct?

Uhm ... yes, but ... there's a time and a place for that, Quasar. This is not the one.

I do not understand.

Rather tell us what **happened** back there.

"Well ... while I was keeping watch, those reptiles started to socialise on the TG-1."

Shoo, you naughty animals!

"They were defecating on the hull! It is not in my program to clean up poop, so I tried to chase them off...

...but, one of them seemingly found my actions annoying."

Help Quasar back to his quarters while I wrap up here. It'll be dark soon.

Will do, Prof.

Here, take back your hand!

As they help Quasar back to the ship...

Psst. Look down – you'll notice something hilarious.

"It looks like Quasar had such a big fright that he couldn't contain himself."

Hie hie-hie

Gmf ... h...he-he

I don't find your "humor" amusing. I am leaking lubricants, idiots.

It's almost as bad as leaking blood to you humans!

{ That is ... very unlike Quasar. }

It looks like Mister Transistor requires repairs on his "brains" too.

That evening...

Professor, the equipment to help fix atmospheric engine 3 will be ready by tomorrow morning. I am just concerned about how the TG-1 is going to take off once we're ready to depart – given the vessel's current inclination.

I've thought about that. We'll take it one step at a time. We'll come up with a plan, I'm sure.

How is Quasar?

Quasar is undertaking repairs on himself, but it also seems like he sustained damage to his personality subroutines. He's developed some rather ... peculiar ... personal traits!

29

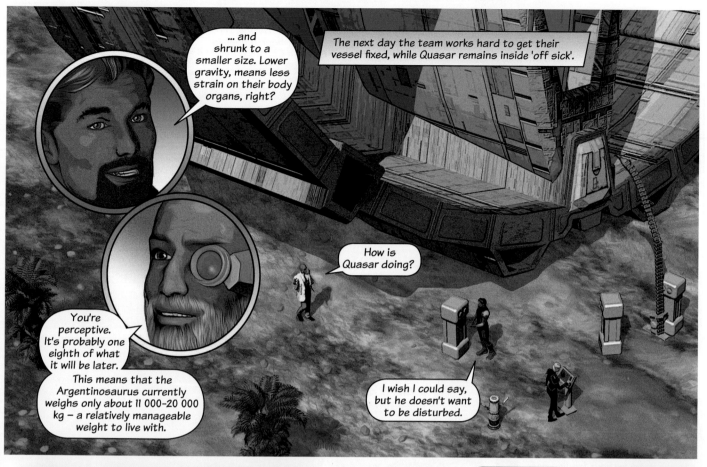

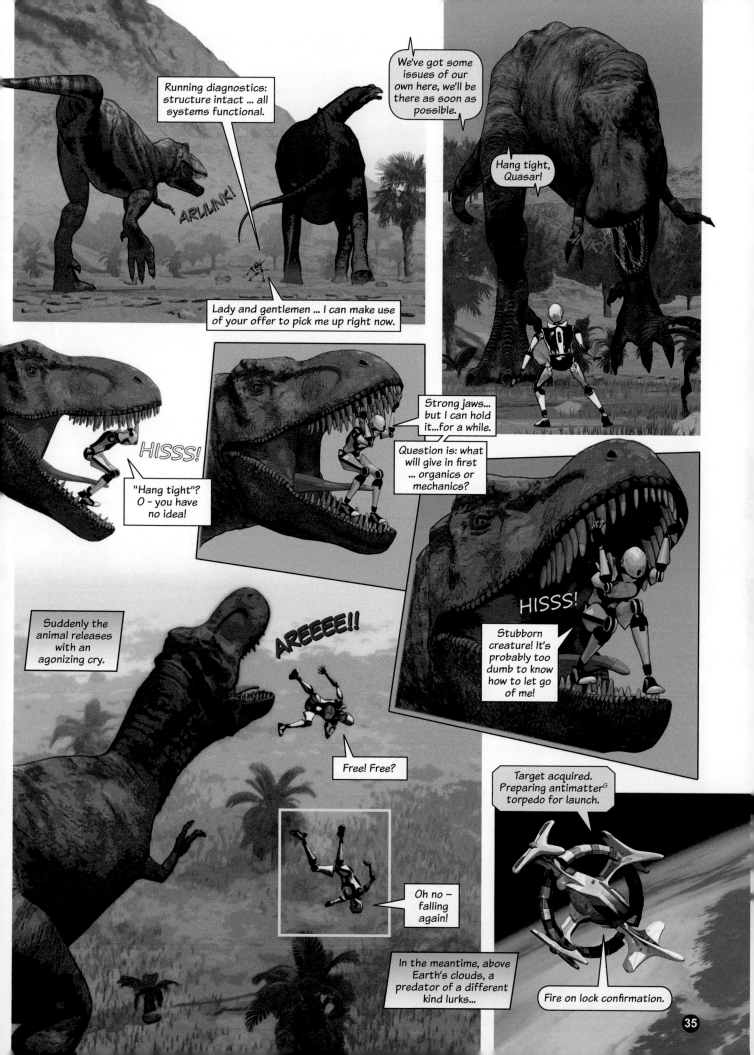

"Locking target ..."

"... locking ..."

"... locking ... locking ..."

"Get it over with, stupid computer!"

"Too much volcanic interference. Abandoning targeting sequence."

Back on the surface, Quasar suddenly realizes why the T-Rex let go of him.

The lava got him! Poor creature, yet with a 99,9% probability, it **saved** me!

He watches as more and more lava comes flowing downhill ...

Ironically ... it may now also lead to my **doom!**

TG-1 – I require your immediate assistance.

One moment, Quasar.

"One moment", they say, but they always expect me to give exact time estimates...

How long is "one moment" TG-1?

S-S-S-SH-S

S-S-S-SH

Quasar – prepare for tractor beam extraction.

Impeccable timing, TG-1.

Somehow I wish they could have found me in a different posture.

Hah! Good thinking, Deon! And luckily, meteor showers of this magnitude are far more common during this time than in our modern era.
Liz, prepare for the jump the moment we're out of this.

But the pursuer hasn't given up yet.

I can see the end of this shower.

Computer, plot a safe course and intercept point for the target as soon as it exits the meteor area.

Course plotted. With target's current trajectory$^G$ and speed, ETA* is 11 seconds.

Engage, max thrust!

Bad news – I don't think Branco's given up yet. His altered course seems to be exploring a way around the meteors.

Deon, do we have an exit strategy?

Exit strategy? I guess ... safe in terms of evading Branco. In terms of flying – not that safe!

And he's gaining speed – fast!

What is it?

The TG-2 will have a tactical advantage soon...

Going straight up – facing the shower head-on.

That sounds too risky.

Deon ...

We'll be in the clear in no time!

... do it.

*Estimated time of arrival

"Sorry, I told ya!"

"Uughh – going to faint!"

"Aaaghh!"

"Here goes – maximum thrust."

Ok, brace yourselves – the g-forces$^G$ could be nasty!

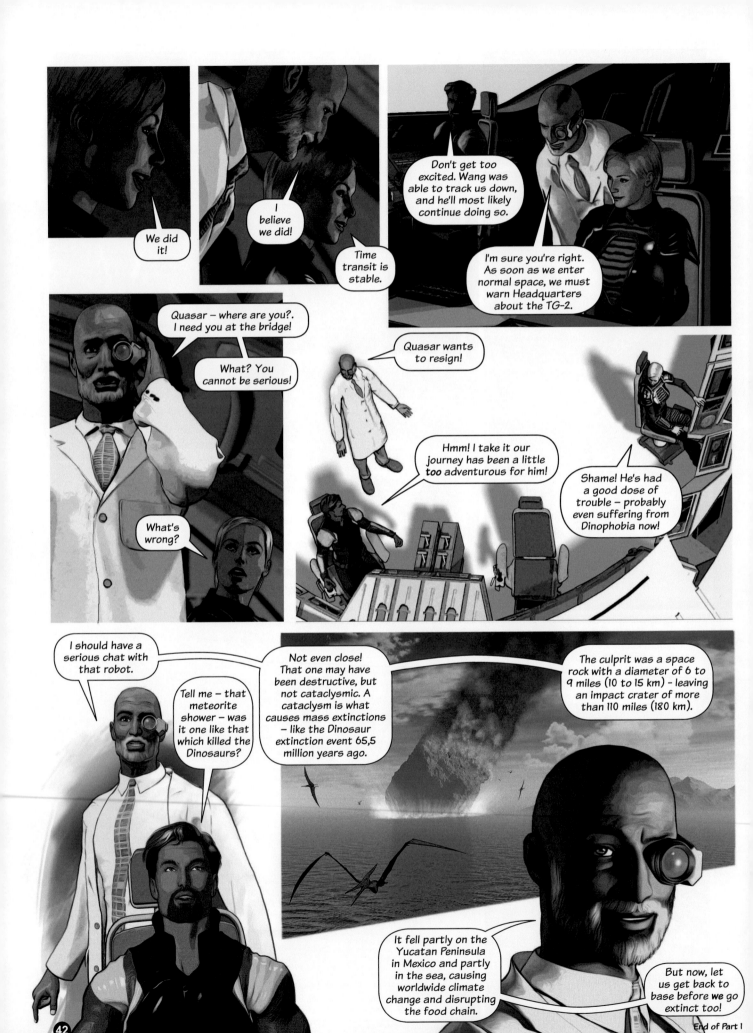

We did it!

I believe we did!

Time transit is stable.

Don't get too excited. Wang was able to track us down, and he'll most likely continue doing so.

I'm sure you're right. As soon as we enter normal space, we must warn Headquarters about the TG-2.

Quasar – where are you?. I need you at the bridge!

What? You cannot be serious!

What's wrong?

Quasar wants to resign!

Hmm! I take it our journey has been a little **too** adventurous for him!

Shame! He's had a good dose of trouble – probably even suffering from Dinophobia now!

I should have a serious chat with that robot.

Tell me – that meteorite shower – was it one like that which killed the Dinosaurs?

Not even close! That one may have been destructive, but not cataclysmic. A cataclysm is what causes mass extinctions – like the Dinosaur extinction event 65,5 million years ago.

The culprit was a space rock with a diameter of 6 to 9 miles (10 to 15 km) - leaving an impact crater of more than 110 miles (180 km).

It fell partly on the Yucatan Peninsula in Mexico and partly in the sea, causing worldwide climate change and disrupting the food chain.

But now, let us get back to base before we go extinct too!

End of Part I

# GLOSSARY

**Antimatter** - Matter composed of subatomic particles (see "Subatomic Particles") that have properties opposing those of normal subatomic particles. Antimatter is the opposite of normal matter. Particles and antiparticles have the same mass but opposite electric charges. When they collide, they annihilate each other and release energy.

**Black Hole** - Sometimes called a "space-time trap", this is an extremely dense region in space in which the gravitational field is so strong that not even light can escape its pull. Anything sucked into a black hole can never escape. At its centre, the normal laws of physics break down. Albert Einstein's theory of general relativity predicted the existence of black holes, long before methods were developed to detect them indirectly – for instance, by their gravitational effects on neighbouring stars and how they deflect the light of far-away objects behind them.

**Celestial Body** - Any natural object that fills space outside of Earth's atmosphere. Also called astronomical objects.

**Coalesce** - To come together to form one mass or whole.

**Cretaceous Period** - Following the Jurassic period in geologic time, the Cretaceous began around 145.5 million years ago and ended about 65.5 million years ago with the mass extinction of the dinosaurs.

**Doppler Effect** - An increase (or decrease) in the frequency of a wavelike signal such as sound or light as the source and the observer move towards (or away from) each other. This effect causes the sudden change in pitch we hear from a passing siren, as well as the red or blue shift in the light spectra of celestial bodies observed by astronomers (see "Red Shift").

**General Relativity** - A well-established theory of physics that has been confirmed experimentally regarding the relationship between space, matter, energy and time. In 1905 Einstein published his Special Theory of Relativity, which reconciled the physics of moving bodies developed by Galileo and Newton with the laws of electromagnetic radiation. It implied that space and time are intertwined (from there the term "space-time") and that the speed of light is constant irrespective of the observer's motion while measuring it.

His Theory of General Relativity, published in 1916, included gravity and used the mathematics of geometry to relate the geometry of space-time to the amount of energy that it contains. Matter does not simply pull on other matter in space (as Newton thought), but rather distorts (or warps) space-time, which in turn affects matter. The amount of distortion is determined by the density of an object. This effect explains gravity – the force of attraction between objects that includes all celestial bodies like planets and their moons that orbit stars (see "Celestial body").

**Genus** - A group of related animals or plants used in biological classification (also called taxonomy) that includes several or many different species.

**G-forces** - Also called surface-contact forces, anything with mass that is under acceleration experiences an increased perception of weight. It is produced by mechanical force (independent of gravity) causing stresses and strains on objects. In aviation it is commonly measured in "g" to describe the increased forces that pilots must overcome to remain conscious if their jet aircraft accelerate rapidly. For instance, fighter pilots must be able to sustain up to 9 g's – this is 9 times their body weight pushing against them.

**Inflation** - The theory of the exponential expansion of space-time during an incredibly short fraction of a second after the Big Bang.

**Inertia** - Isaac Newton's first law of motion. It refers to the resistance of an object to any external force to its state of motion (whether it is moving or stationary). If too much of an external force is applied too quickly, it can be thrown off-balance or its structure may be damaged.

**Laws of Physics** - Statements that describe the behaviour and motions of things in nature, often expressed mathematically. These laws are based on repeatable scientific experiments and observations and are universal (i.e. they appear to apply throughout the Universe). There are two categories for these laws: classical physics, which deal with the observable world; and atomic physics, which describe the interactions between elementary and subatomic particles.

**Neural** - Generally refers to the nervous system, the part of an animal's body which transmits electric signals and coordinates actions between body parts. Vertebrate species with a backbone, or spinal column, have a central nervous system (CNS) consisting of the brain and spinal cord, and the peripheral nervous system (PNS) of connected nerves that reach every part of the body.

Neural design principles are being replicated in computer science, because artificial neural networks (ANNs) hold promise for self-learning (instead of fixed programming). This is the future for artificial intelligence.

As you might have guessed, Quasar's ANN has a specialized interface in one of his fingertips, enabling him to connect with biological neural networks as well! This feature sometimes makes the Time Glider team uncomfortable, with Prof Patel eager to find out if it was part of Quasar's original design.

# GLOSSARY

**Plate Tectonics** - Earth's crust is made of plates that move around on the mantle beneath it. Where the plates meet, their relative motion may cause earthquakes, volcanic activity, mountain forming and oceanic trench forming. The concept of continental drift (i.e. how the Earth originally had one super continent that split over time into all the main continents of today), builds on this model.

**Protoplanetary Disk** - A rotating circumstellar disk of dense gas surrounding a young newly formed star. "Proto" means first" or "earliest", thus implying that planets are yet to form.

**Quantum Physics** - Describes the behaviour of atoms and subatomic particles (see "Subatomic Particles"). It even helps to explain nuclear fusion processes inside stars.

**Quetzalcoatlus** - A flying reptile that existed 220-65 million years ago. It had an estimated wingspan of 30-35 feet (9 - 11 m) – the size of a typical World War 2 fighter aircraft!

**Radiometric Dating** - Also termed radioactive dating. A technique used to determine the age of geological materials such as rocks, or organic materials containing carbon. Radioactive elements decay at different rates, so the amount of a decaying element left in a material can help determine its age. There are various dating techniques - each relevant for a specific type of material or situation. Some of the common ones are: Carbon-14, Uranium-lead, Potassium-argon, Uranium-thorium, etc.

**Red Shift** - In the visible portion of the electromagnetic spectrum (white light), blue has the highest frequency and red has the lowest. When stars or galaxies are moving away from us, their light waves are stretched into lower frequencies or longer wavelengths, and we say that the light is red shifted. If they are moving towards us, the colour shifts to blue. Astronomers use this knowledge to help explain our expanding Universe.

**Sauropods** - Plant-eating dinosaurs with very long necks, long tails, small heads in comparison to the rest of their bodies and pillar-like legs. Notable for their enormous sizes, well-known sauropods are Argentinosaurus, Apatosaurus and Brachiosaurus. A new species excavated between 2012 and 2013 in Argentina, named Patagotitan mayorum, is the largest fossil find to date. It measures 122 feet (37 m) long and 20 feet (6 m) high at the shoulder!

**Solar Nebula** - Our solar system began forming within a cloud of interstellar dust and hydrogen gas. The cloud contracted under its own gravity and our Sun formed in the hot dense center. The remainder of the cloud formed a swirling disk called the solar nebula, out of which planets, moons, etc. formed.

**Stellar** - Anything related to, or consisting of, stars.

**Subatomic Particles** - The smallest components of an atom, with protons and neutrons making up the nucleus and electrons orbiting it. Some of these particles, such as protons and neutrons, consist of even smaller sub-particles, such as quarks and neutrinos. These, along with electrons, belong to a class called "elementary particles" because they are not made up from any smaller units.

**Supernova** - A gigantic stellar explosion so bright that it can briefly outshine an entire galaxy before fading from view over several weeks or months.

**Tachyon Particle** - A hypothetical subatomic particle that always moves faster than light. Physicists like Albert Einstein and Richard C. Tolman noted that if faster-than-light particles existed, general relativity implied that they could be used to communicate backwards in time.

**Trajectory** - The path followed by a flying projectile, satellite or rocket which is under the influence of given forces.

**T-rex** - Tyrannosaurus rex, "king of the dinosaurs". One of the largest meat-eating dinosaurs of the Cretaceous Period, measuring 12 meters (40 feet) and weighing 4-7 tonnes. It has been outclassed in terms of size by newer fossil finds of meat-eaters such as Spinosaurus and Giganotosaurus.

**Troposphere** - The lowest portion of Earth's atmosphere, extending up to altitudes between 5 and 9 miles (8 and 14 km). Here, all weather takes place.

**Wormhole** - A hypothetical "bridge" or shortcut in the structure of space-time that potentially links parts of the universe that are far apart.

# BIBLIOGRAPHY

**BOOKS:**

Jane Bingham, Fiona Chandler and Sam Taplin, *The Usborne internet-linked encyclopedia of world history* (Usborne Publishing, 2001)
Gordon Fraser and Egil Lillestol, *The Search for Infinity: Solving the Mysteries of the Universe* (Facts on File, 1995)
Richard Moody, *Dinofile*, (London: Ticktock Books Ltd, 2009)
Martin Redfern, *The Kingfisher young people's book of space* (Kingfisher, 1998)
Robert P. Yamin and Terri Monaghan, *Dinosaur Mystery Solved* (U.S.: Book World Press, 1989)

**INTERNET SOURCES:**

www.britannica.com/science
www.dinopedia.wikia.com
www.dummies.com/education/science/physics/
www.einstein-online.info

www.newdinosaurs.com
www.physicsoftheuniverse.com
www.sci-news.com/paleontology/
www.wikipedia.com

To order additional copies of this book, contact:
Xlibris
AU TFN: 1 800 844 927 (Toll Free inside Australia)
AU Local: 0283 108 187 (+61 2 8310 8187 from outside Australia)
www.xlibris.com.au
Orders@Xlibris.com.au

ISBN:    Softcover        978-1-9845-0638-2
         EBook            978-1-9845-0639-9

Print information available on the last page

Rev. date: 06/22/2020

Printed in the United States
By Bookmasters